*A book
is a present you can open
again and again.*

THIS BOOK BELONGS TO

_____

FROM

_____

Hansel and Gretel

Little Red-Cap

The Musicians of Bremen

The Brothers Grimm

Illustrated by Alexander Koshkin

TREASURE TREE™

World Book, Inc.
a Scott Fetzer company
Chicago   London   Sydney   Toronto

Hansel and Gretel

Once upon a time, at the edge of a great forest, there lived a poor woodcutter, his wife, and the children of his first marriage, Hansel and Gretel. They had little enough to eat in the best of times. But when famine caused even greater scarcity, the woodcutter could not provide his family with their daily bread. One night the woodcutter could not sleep. He asked his wife, "How will we feed our children when we haven't enough food for ourselves?"

"Listen, husband," the wife replied. "At sunrise tomorrow, we will lead the children deep into the woods. There, we will light a fire, give them one last slice of bread, go off to work, and leave them. They will never find their way home, and so our troubles will be gone."

"No, wife, that is unthinkable!" the woodcutter exclaimed. "I could not leave my dear children alone in the forest to become supper for some wild beast."

"If you do not take my advice," the wife replied,

"all four of us will die of hunger. Why, you might as well start smoothing the planks for the coffins." She carried on this way until, at last, the man gave in.

He shook his head and lamented, "I am sorry that I cannot do better for my children."

Because of their hunger, Hansel and Gretel had been unable to sleep either, so they heard what their stepmother said to their father. Gretel turned to Hansel and sobbed, "This is the end of us."

"Hush, Gretel," Hansel consoled, "Do not despair. I will think of something." He waited until his parents were finally asleep. Then he got dressed, opened the door, and crept outside. In the moonlit night, the white pebbles in the yard gleamed as brightly as freshly minted coins. Hansel stuffed as many pebbles into his pockets as he could. Then he went back inside. "Do not worry, dear little sister," he said to Gretel. "God will not abandon us. Go to sleep." Then he climbed into bed.

At the crack of dawn, even before the sun rose in the sky, the stepmother awakened the children. "Wake up, lazybones," she called. "It's time to go to the forest to gather wood." She handed each child a slice of bread and said, "Here is something for dinner. Don't eat it too early, for there is no more."

Gretel tucked both pieces into her apron pocket because Hansel's were filled with pebbles. Then the family set out into the forest. As they walked, Hansel stopped and turned his eyes homeward. He did this several times. Finally, his father called to him, "Hansel, why do you constantly lag behind? Eyes ahead—hurry along."

"Papa," replied Hansel. "I am looking at my kitten on the roof. It is mewing good-by to me."

"Silly," scolded the stepmother. "That is not your

kitten on the roof. It is sunshine on the chimney."

However, Hansel was not really looking at his cat. Each time he turned around, he dropped one of the pebbles on the path.

When they were deep in the forest, their father said, "Children, make haste. Gather a pile of wood, and I will light a fire so that you will not be cold." Hansel and Gretel gathered a great heap of dry twigs. The fire was lit, and when it was blazing, the stepmother said, "Now you children stay near the fire and rest. We are going deeper into the forest to chop wood. When we are done, we will return for you."

Hansel and Gretel stayed by the fire. They could hear the sound of an ax nearby and so believed that their father was nearby. But it was not an ax that they heard. Their father had tied a dead branch to the tree. As it banged about in the wind, it pounded against the tree. For a long time, the children waited. Eventually, their eyelids grew heavy and they fell asleep. When they awoke, it was night. Gretel began to cry, "We will never get out of the woods."

Hansel comforted her, "When the moon rises, we will find our way."

When the moon shone bright, Hansel took his sister by the hand and followed the pebbles. They sparkled like newly minted coins in the moonlight, marking the path home. They walked all through the night, and as day was breaking, they found themselves

at home. They knocked, and their stepmother opened the door. As soon as she saw who it was, she began to shout, "You naughty children, why did you sleep out all night in the woods? We thought that you had run away." Their father, however, rejoiced, because he was sorry he had left them alone.

Some time went by, and another famine began. One night, the children heard their stepmother say to their father, "There is nothing left to eat. We must get rid of the children. We will take them even deeper into the forest so that they will never be able to find the way out. There is nothing else to do."

The father was heartsick. "It would be better to share our last mouthful with the children," he said. But his wife, knowing that he had given in to her before, gave him no peace until he did so again.

Hansel and Gretel were awake and so heard every word. Once again, when the grown-ups were asleep, Hansel crept out of bed. He intended to gather pebbles once more, but his stepmother had locked the door and he was unable to open it. Still, he comforted Gretel, "Do not cry. God will care for us."

Early the next morning, they were awakened by their stepmother. She gave them each a slice of bread, smaller than before. As they walked into the forest, Hansel tore his bread and every now and then stopped to drop a crumb onto the path.

"Hansel, why do you stop and look back?" asked his father. "You'd best keep up."

"But father, I am looking at my pigeon up on the roof," replied Hansel. "See it cooing good-by to us?"

"Silly," reproached the stepmother. "That is not your pigeon. It is the sun's rays on the roof."

They walked on, and bit by bit, Hansel dropped every crumb of bread on the path. The children were

led to a place deeper in the forest than they had ever been. Their father built them a fire and their stepmother said, "Stay here. When you feel tired, rest. We are going to chop wood. When we are done, we will return for you."

At midday, Gretel shared her bread with Hansel since he had dropped his along the way. Then they fell asleep. Evening came, but no one came to fetch them. When they awoke in the middle of the night, Hansel comforted his sister. "Gretel, just wait until the moon

rises. Then we will be able to see the breadcrumbs. They will show us our way home."

When the moon was high, they set off, but they could not find a single crumb of bread. The thousands of birds that fly through the forests and fields had come and eaten it. Hansel said to Gretel, "Never mind. We will find our way home." But they did not. They walked and walked all night and the next day, from dawn to dusk, and still they could not find a way out of the woods. They grew hungrier and hungrier. All they found to eat were a few berries, which they picked from the bushes. When they were too weary to move, they lay down beneath a tree and went to sleep.

Three days had passed and Hansel and Gretel had only managed to wander deeper and deeper into

the forest. It was clear that if they did not find
something to eat soon, they would die of starvation.
At midday, the children saw a beautiful bird perched
on a branch. It was as white as snow and it sang so
prettily that Hansel and Gretel stopped to listen.
When the song was done, the snow-white bird flew
away. The spellbound children followed it. The bird
landed on the roof of a little cottage. The children saw
that the cottage was made of bread, the roof was
made of cake, and the windows were made of icing.

    "Let's help ourselves to a lovely lunch,"
exclaimed Hansel. "I'll have a piece of the roof. You
try a piece of the sugar icing window." Hansel broke
off a piece of the roof and took a big bite. Gretel
began to devour a slab of sugar icing.

Suddenly a voice from inside the cottage called,
> *"I hear the nibbling of a mouse.*
> *Who's that nibbling at my house?"*

The children called back,
> *"It's just the wind, the wind so mild,*
> *Soft and sweet as a heavenly child."*

Then they carried on eating, giving not a second thought to the voice from within.

Each chunk that Hansel broke off the roof was larger than the one before. Gretel removed an entire windowpane and began eating it eagerly. Then the front door burst open. An old woman leaning on a walking stick came out of the cottage. Hansel and Gretel got such a fright that they let the treats in their hands fall to the ground. But the woman shook her head and said, "Dear children, what brings you here? Come inside with me. No harm will befall you."

Taking their hands, she led them inside. She served them dinner, with milk and pancakes, honey and nuts. Then she made two clean beds. When Hansel and Gretel lay down, they thought they were in heaven.

The old lady seemed very kind, but she was really a witch. She had built the sugar-loaf cottage just to trap unsuspecting children. Whenever she managed to catch one, she would kill and cook the child for her supper. It was a day of feasting for her.

Now witches do not have keen eyesight, but they have a keen sense of smell. Like animals, they can sniff out humans close by. When Hansel and Gretel had neared the cottage, the witch had let out an evil laugh and promised herself, "Once these two are in my power, they will not escape me."

The next morning, the witch awoke before Hansel and Gretel. She watched them as they

slumbered. As she admired their plump, rosy cheeks, she muttered to herself, "What an excellent meal they'll make." Then she grabbed Hansel in her scrawny hands, pulled him out of bed, dragged him across the floor, and threw him into a cage. She locked the cage with a steel bar. Hansel could cry for help as much as he liked, but it would do him no good. The witch returned to Gretel and shook her until she was awake.

"Get up, you lazy girl!" she screamed. "Fetch some water and cook something nice for your brother. He's in the cage and must be fattened up. When he is nice and plump, I shall eat him."

Gretel burst into tears, but crying was useless. She had to do what the witch ordered. In the days that followed, Hansel ate excellent meals, while Gretel was lucky to get a few leftovers. Each morning, the old witch hobbled over to the cage and commanded, "Hansel, stick out your finger. I want to see how fat you are." But Hansel did not stick out a finger. Instead, he pushed a bone through the bars. The witch's eyesight was so weak that she could not see that she was being tricked. She was amazed that the boy was not growing fatter. After four weeks, Hansel seemed to be as thin as ever, but she decided that she could not wait.

"Run and fetch water, Gretel," she called. "Be he fat or thin, tomorrow I will have Hansel for supper."

Ah, how hopeless Gretel felt as she went to the well. Her tears were like rain. She prayed, "Dear God, help us. If the wild animals had devoured us in the forest, at least we would have died together."

"Save your tears," the witch said. "They'll not do you any good."

Early the next morning, Gretel was forced to get up, hang a pot of water on the chain, and light the fire. "First of all," said the witch, "we shall bake some bread. I have already heated the oven and prepared the dough." She pushed Gretel toward the oven, where the flames were already burning fiercely. "Climb in," she ordered, "see if it is hot enough to put the bread in."

Gretel realized that if she climbed into the oven the witch would slam the door behind her. She, too, would be baked and eaten. "I do not know what you mean. How do I get inside?" Gretel asked.

"Silly goose," replied the witch. "The oven door is big enough even for me to get inside." To prove her point, the witch hobbled there and stuck her head into the oven. At once, Gretel gave her a great shove that made her fall into the oven. Gretel slammed the door and bolted it. Oh, how the witch began to shriek, and what horrid screams! But Gretel ran away, leaving the witch to burn.

Gretel rushed over to Hansel, opened the cage, and cried, "Hansel, we are free. The wicked old witch is dead!" Hansel sprung from the cage like a freed bird. How happy they were! Joyfully, they hugged and kissed each other. With nothing left to fear, they

poked around in every corner of the witch's cottage. They found boxes overflowing with pearls and other precious stones. "These are even prettier than the pebbles," Hansel said, stuffing his pockets. Saying, "I want to take some home," Gretel filled her apron.

"Let's go," said Hansel. "We have to get out of these woods of the witch." So Hansel and Gretel set off for home. After they had walked for a while, they came to a wide river. "We cannot get across," moaned Hansel. "I do not see a bridge or any way over."

"And there is no boat to carry us," added Gretel. "But look over there! I see a duck," exclaimed Gretel. "If I ask her nicely, she will carry us over." As she spoke, Gretel's sweet voice reached the duck, who swam over to the children.

Hansel sat on her back and told Gretel to get on behind him. Gretel, however, took pity on the duck and said, "No, it would be too heavy a weight to bear. Let her take one at a time."

So that is what the kind bird did. When Hansel and Gretel were safe on the other side, they noticed that the woods became more familiar with every step. Upon reaching home, they burst in the door and threw their arms around their father's neck.

The man had had no peace since abandoning his children in the forest. What is more, his wife had died. Then Gretel opened her apron. Pearls and jewels spilled onto the floor. Hansel emptied his pockets, too. And so the family's suffering came to an end and they all lived a long and happy life together.

Little Red-Cap

Once upon a time there was a little girl so sweet that everyone who knew her loved her. She was especially adored by her grandmother. The old woman once gave her granddaughter a red velvet cap. The little girl loved the red cap so much that she wore it wherever she went. Everyone noticed how well the red cap suited the girl and, since she was never seen without it, she soon became known as Little Red-Cap.

One morning, Little Red-Cap's mother called for her. "Grandmother is not well," she began. "I want you to take her the cake I baked and a bottle of cider. Mind you, do not stray from the path."

"I promise," replied Little Red-Cap.

The girl's grandmother lived deep in the forest, a long walk from the village. As Little Red-Cap entered the woods, she met a wolf. Now she did not know what a wicked creature this wolf was, so she wasn't afraid.

"Good morning, Little Red-Cap," said the wolf. "Where are you going in such a hurry?"

"To my grandmother's house."

"Pray tell, what are you carrying in your basket?"

Little Red-Cap answered, "Cake and cider for my grandmother; she is not well."

"How thoughtful," said the wolf. "And where does your grandmother live?"

"A bit farther, under the three great oaks. Surely you must have seen her hut."

The wolf's mind was spinning with plans. "This tender little girl would be tasty. She will be more juicy than her grandmother, but if I am crafty, I can have both of them." As he walked along beside Little Red-Cap, he said, "Do you see the lovely flowers? Why not

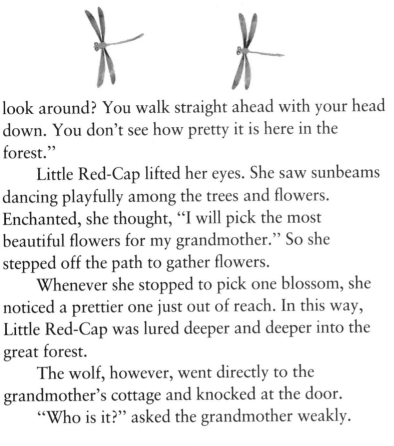

look around? You walk straight ahead with your head
down. You don't see how pretty it is here in the
forest."

Little Red-Cap lifted her eyes. She saw sunbeams
dancing playfully among the trees and flowers.
Enchanted, she thought, "I will pick the most
beautiful flowers for my grandmother." So she
stepped off the path to gather flowers.

Whenever she stopped to pick one blossom, she
noticed a prettier one just out of reach. In this way,
Little Red-Cap was lured deeper and deeper into the
great forest.

The wolf, however, went directly to the
grandmother's cottage and knocked at the door.

"Who is it?" asked the grandmother weakly.

Disguising his voice, the wolf answered, "It is I, Little Red-Cap. Please open the door."

"Pull up the latch," said the grandmother. "I am too weak to get out of bed."

The wolf pulled up the latch. The door opened. And without a word the wolf ran to the bed and swallowed the grandmother in one mouthful! Then he put on a nightgown and nightcap and got into the bed.

Meanwhile, Little Red-Cap was still busy picking flowers. It wasn't until her arms were full that she remembered why she had begun to pick them. Then she hurried to the cottage. She was surprised to find the door open. As she entered, a strange feeling of fear came over her. "How odd," she thought. "Usually I feel safe the moment I enter Granny's." She said loudly, "Good morning!" There was no answer. So she went to the bed. There lay her grandmother with her nightcap pulled low, looking very strange.

"Grandmother, what big ears you have," cried Little Red-Cap.

"All the better to hear you with, my dear."

"Grandmother, what big eyes you have!"

"All the better to see you with, my dear."

"Grandmother, what big hands you have!"

"All the better to hold you with, my dear."

"Grandmother, what a terribly big mouth you have!"

"All the better to eat you with, my dear."

And with these words, the wolf leapt out of bed and swallowed Little Red-Cap whole.

Feeling rather full, the wolf went back to bed and was soon snoring loudly. Just then a hunter passed the cottage and heard the snores. He thought, "What a strange sound! I'd better see if the old woman is well." Going in, he saw the wolf in the bed. "At last I've

found you, you old scoundrel!" he exclaimed.

The hunter was about to shoot when he had an odd thought. Perhaps the wolf had swallowed the old lady, and perhaps he could save her. He picked up a pair of scissors and began cutting the wolf's stomach while the beast slept. After a few snips, he saw a red cap. After a few more snips, Little Red-Cap leapt out, crying, "What a fright I've had!"

Then out came her grandmother, too, still alive.

The hunter sent Little Red-Cap to gather heavy

stones. He put the stones into the wolf's stomach and stitched it up. When the wolf awoke, he tried to run. The stones, however, were so heavy that he fell down dead.

Little Red-Cap, her grandmother, and the hunter were overjoyed. The hunter skinned the wolf and went off with the hide. The grandmother ate the cake and drank the cider that Little Red-Cap had brought, and she soon felt strong again. Little Red-Cap declared, "Never again will I leave the path and go into the woods alone against my mother's wishes!"

The Musicians of Bremen

Long ago, a man owned a donkey. For years, the donkey had carried his master's sacks of grain to the mill without complaint. Now, however, the donkey had grown too old to work. The donkey saw that his master was preparing to put an end to him. So he ran away. He trotted down the road to the town of Bremen. There, he thought, he could join the town band.

After a while, he came upon a hunting dog. The dog was panting as if he had just run his last race. "What is the matter, good dog?" inquired the donkey.

"It's a pity," replied the dog. "Now that I am old, I am no longer able to hunt. I overheard my master say that he planned to kill me. I fled to save my life. But now how will I earn my living?"

"Listen to me," said the donkey. "I am on my way to Bremen to become a musician. Come with me and join the band. I'll play the lute and you can beat the drum."

The dog accepted, and the two went off together. A little farther along, they came upon a sorrowful cat.

"Swallowed something that disagreed with you, have you, cat?" inquired the donkey.

"How can I be happy when my life is in danger?" the cat answered. "Now that I am old, my teeth are no longer strong, and I prefer to nap in front of a cozy fire rather than rush about chasing mice. So my mistress intends to drown me. I managed to get away, it's true, but now what am I to do?"

"Come with us to Bremen," suggested the donkey. "You know something about night serenades. Why not join with us in the town band?"

The cat thought that was a fine idea, and the three went off together. Farther on, they came upon a rooster on a gate, crowing at the top of his voice.

"Hey," brayed the donkey. "Are you trying to crow your head off? What is this all about?"

"I'm forecasting good weather," replied the rooster. "Today will be a wonderful day—good for drying the wash. But tomorrow, Sunday, guests are coming, and my mistress has given the cook orders to turn me into the main course. They will kill me tonight. I crow now, for soon I will crow no more."

"Well, rooster," began the donkey, "why don't you join us? We are on our way to Bremen to become musicians. There you will be met with something better than death. You've got a fine voice. If we band together, we're sure to find employment."

The rooster liked the idea, and the four of them went off together. Now, the walk to Bremen was more than a day's walk, so the friends went into the woods to find a place to rest. The donkey and the dog lay down under a tree, while the cat and rooster nestled in the branches. The rooster went all the way to the top of the tree. Before he settled down to sleep, he looked all around. He saw a light shining in the distance. The rooster called down to his friends that there must be a house nearby. "Well," said the donkey, "let's go and have a look. These lodgings are none too comfortable."

The dog drooled at the thought of bones with some meat on them, and the cat imagined herself sleeping in front of the hearth. So the donkey, the dog, the cat, and the rooster all set off together to find the light.

At length, the four friends arrived at a lighted house. Obviously, someone was inside. Being tallest, the donkey went to the window and peered in.

"What do you see, old donkey?" the dog whispered.

"What do I see?" replied the donkey. "I see a

table spread with all sorts of good things, and thieves sitting around it, enjoying themselves."

"If only it were ours," sighed the rooster.

"Ah, to be inside," agreed the donkey.

With that, the four friends discussed how to get the robbers out of the house. At last they had a plan. The donkey put his forefeet on the window sill. The dog jumped onto his back. The cat climbed onto the dog's back. And the rooster flew up and perched on the cat's head. When all were ready, the friends burst into song. The donkey brayed, the dog barked, the cat

meowed, and the rooster crowed. Then they tumbled into the room with a great crashing roar amid the sound of shattering glass.

At the horrible racket, the robbers leapt to their feet. Believing that ghosts had come, they fled in terror.

The four companions sat at the table and ate as if they had not seen food for a month. When they had eaten their fill, the musicians put out the candles. Each found a place to make a bed, according to his own idea of comfort. The donkey lay down on the straw in the courtyard. The dog curled up behind the door. The cat lay on the warm ashes near the fireplace. And the rooster perched on a wooden beam. They had walked far and were soon asleep.

The robbers had been watching the house. Shortly after midnight, they saw the lights go out. When all seemed quiet, the leader said, "We should not have let ourselves be frightened off." He sent one of his men to have a closer look.

The robber fellow went to the house and found that all was quiet. He crept into the kitchen to light a fire. Seeing the glowing eyes of the cat, he mistook them for smoldering embers. He poked his match at them. The cat sprang up in a fury and leapt at his face, hissing and scratching wildly. The terrified robber fled toward the back door. But the dog, lying there, jumped up and bit his leg. As he ran screaming into the courtyard, the donkey kicked him with his hind

legs. The ruckus woke the rooster and he began to crow, "Cock-a-doodle-doo!"

The robber ran back to his captain with what legs he had. "In that house," he stammered, "there is a terrible witch. She blew poison in my face and scratched me with her nails. By the door, a man with a knife stabbed me in the leg. Outside, a monster beat me with a club. On high, a judge shouted, 'Bring that villain to me, do!' I was lucky to escape."

From then on, the robbers did not dare to set foot in the house again. But the four musicians of Bremen found it so comfortable that they are living there still.

To Parents

Children delight in hearing and reading fairy tales. "Hansel and Gretel," "Little Red-Cap," and "The Musicians of Bremen" will provide your child with entertaining stories as well as a bridge into learning some important concepts. Here are a few easy and natural ways your child can express feelings and understandings about the stories. You know your child and can best judge which ideas he or she will enjoy most.

Encourage your child to draw a picture from a favorite story in the book, such as the witch's house in "Hansel and Gretel." Work together with different materials to decorate the picture. Some useful objects are yarn, string, beads, buttons, and pieces of candy. If you've selected the witch's house, you and your child can enjoy making a real gingerbread house of icing, gingerbread cookies, and any of the materials.

You and your child may enjoy creating a puppet show from any of the stories in the book. For example, for "Little Red-Cap," help your child make stick puppets of the five characters. Turn a table on its side to make a stage. Then retell the story for your "family audience," taking turns handling the puppets and voicing their lines.

Many fairy-tale characters follow paths to certain places. For example, Hansel and Gretel follow a path into the woods. You and your child can turn these paths into games. For "Hansel and Gretel," draw a large picture of the forest to make a game board. Add a winding path of double squares from the woodcutter's house to the witch's house. Place two small markers, such as coins, on the first two squares at the woodcutter's house. Write 1, 2, or 3 on small pieces of paper and put the pieces into a bag. Take turns picking a number and moving your markers that many spaces along the path.

Fairy tales don't have to stop at the end of the story. You and your child can enjoy new chapters that you make up. For example, start a new chapter for "The Musicians of Bremen" by asking your child, "What do you think will happen next for the musicians?" Help by giving a first line such as, "One day, there was a knock at the door of the animals' new home." Write down your child's new chapter, or ask for a written chapter if your child already writes.